Jerome the Stone

By Dorothy Shaw

Doodle and Peck Publishing
P.O. Box 852105
Yukon, OK 73085
405.354.7422
www.doodleandpeck.com

(Temporary Cataloging Information)
Shaw, Dorothy
Jerome the Stone/by Dorothy Shaw/illustrated by Dorothy Shaw
Summary: Jerome wanted to see the world. He really wanted to
fly. His chance came when a boy picked him up and flung him
high into the sky. He loved it. After he landed, he looked
forward to more adventures the next day.
ISBN: 978-1-7327713-3-8 (hard copy)
ISBN: 978-1-7327713-2-1 (soft copy)

1. Atmosphere   2. Rocks   3. Stones   4. I. Dorothy Shaw, Ill.

E

Library of Congress Control Number: 2019930316

Dedicated to Eva
and her trusty sidekick, Joel.
You guys rock.

Special thanks to Ron,
for his patient support and editing.
And for making me a slingshot.

Simple activities designed to help parents and/or caregivers participate in, and support, a child's literacy skills and educational goals:

Linking
to
Literacy

- **Easiest**: **On the cover, point to** the letter **Oo. As you read the story together, count how many** O**s are on each page.**

- **More Difficult**: **Discuss the** opposites **to these words in the book: cool, out, hungry, up, right, dark, tiny, soft, below.**

- Challenging: **The** vowel pattern VCV **usually means the first vowel makes its** *long* **sound, or says"its own name." Find three words in the book with this vowel pattern.**

*Free, printable resources may be found at www.doodleandpeck.com. Click on the Linking to Literacy Resources tab and print off as many activities as you need.

Jerome the Stone yawned
in the cool morning shade.

Ants marched in and out of tunnels. Worms peeked out of the damp dirt. Slugs left silver trails, grasshoppers hopped, and lady bugs explored. Nearby, a preying mantis watched them with hungry eyes.

Jerome gazed at the butterflies,
birds, and bees riding on the breeze.

"What do they see?" he wondered.
"I want to fly, too!"

Jerome knew he
could not fly like a bird...
or hop like a grasshopper...
or fly in an airplane.

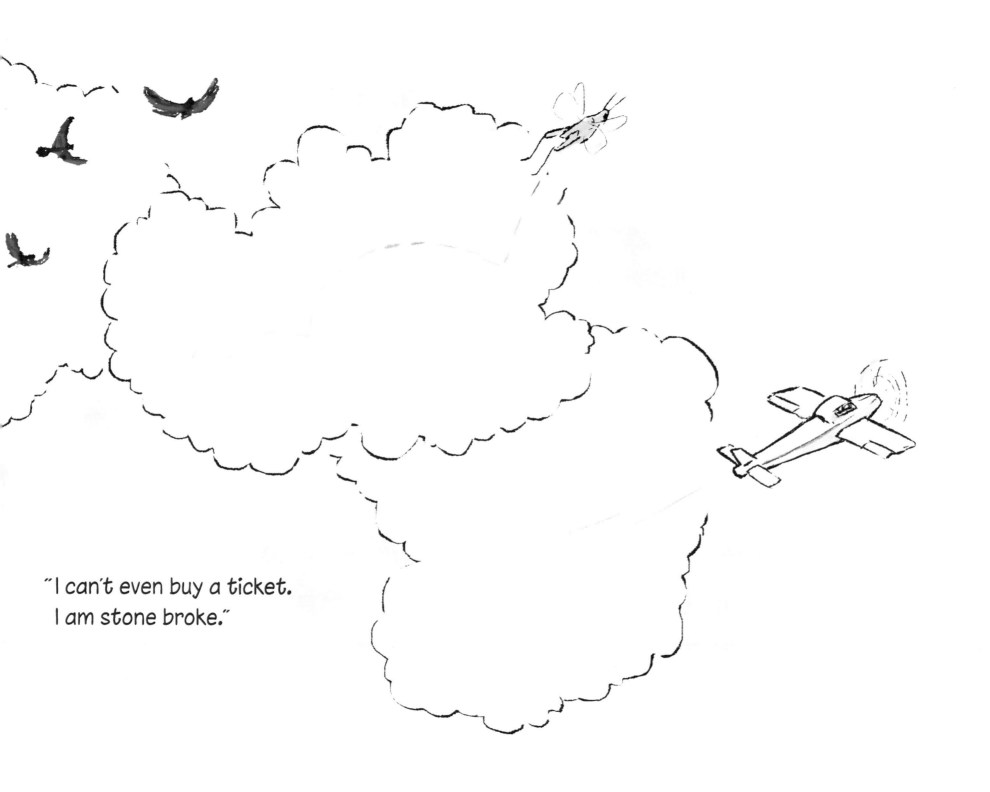

"I can't even buy a ticket.
I am stone broke."

But Jerome
just had to try.

He snorted,
grunted, and
groaned.

He leaned to the left.

He leaned to the right.
Nothing. Nada.

He tried to rock and roll.
Zip. Zilch.

He hadn't budged one bit.
"Awww... Who am I kidding?
I'll never be able to..."

THWACK!

Without any warning, Jerome was soaring through the air.

THUNK.

He landed on his head.
"I WAS flying," he thought.
"How did that happen?"

The boy reached down
and snatched up Jerome.
"Perfect," the boy muttered.
"Just the right size.
Just the right shape."
He dropped Jerome
into his pocket.

It was warm and dark, but
Jerome felt a tiny bit scared.

A few minutes later a hand plucked
him out of the pocket and wrapped
him in a piece of soft leather.

"Ooooh," thought Jerome.
"This is nice." He settled in for a nap.

But suddenly...

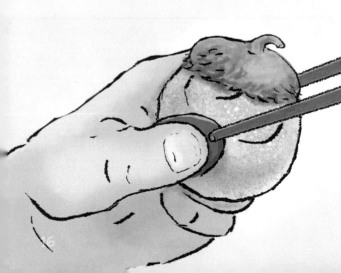

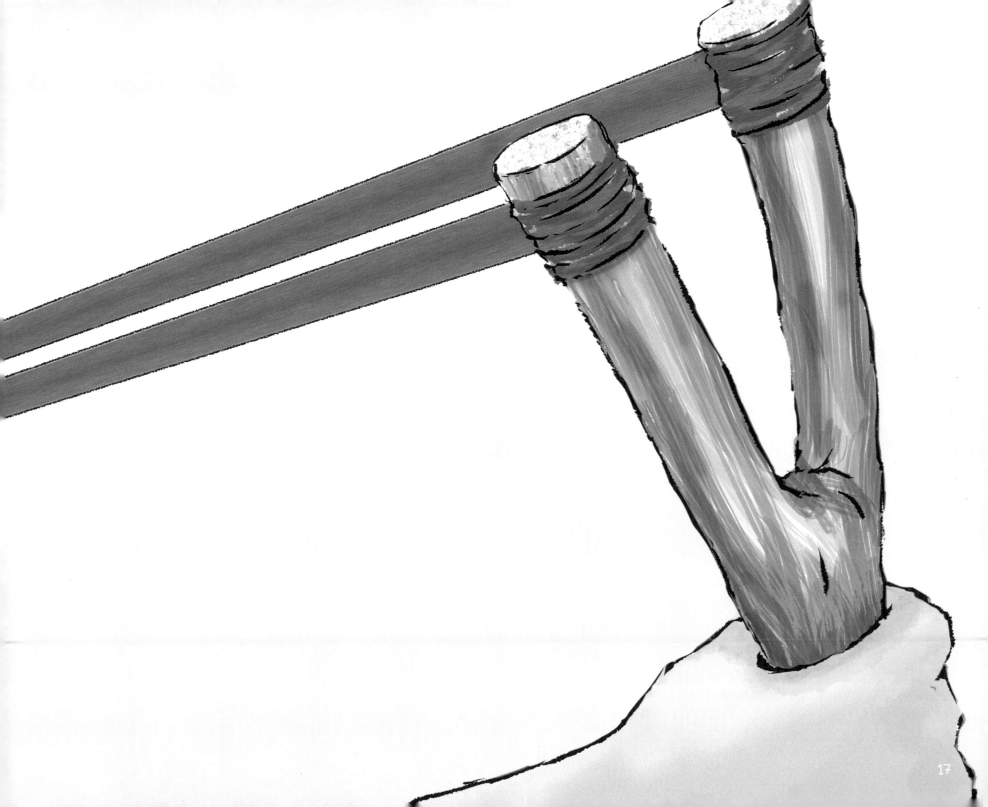

...*SWISH!*

Jerome shot higher than
a kite! He glanced back and
spied the boy, far below.

YEOOOOOW!

"I'm really flying!
Goodbye, dirt.
Goodbye, grass."

He rose higher and higher,
over patchwork fields,
a speeding train, and
even a tiny airplane.

HE BURST

THROUGH THE CLOUDS . . .

...then floated in silence.